small

gina perry

little bee books

🐝 little bee books

An imprint of Bonnier Publishing USA
251 Park Avenue South, New York, NY 10010
Copyright © 2017 by Gina Perry
All rights reserved, including the right of reproduction in whole or in part in any form.
LITTLE BEE BOOKS is a trademark of Bonnier Publishing USA, and associated
colophon is a trademark of Bonnier Publishing USA.
Library of Congress Cataloging-in-Publication Data is available upon request.
Manufactured in China   HH 0517
First Edition   10 9 8 7 6 5 4 3 2 1
ISBN 978-1-4998-0401-0

littlebeebooks.com
bonnierpublishingusa.com

For Mom and Dad
from their smallest girl

The city is big
and I am small.

I look small.
Wide street. Tall buildings.

I walk small.
Noisy cars. Speeding bikes.

I talk small.
Long line. Huge food.

I eat small.
Big bench. Tiny bites.

I am small.

Until . . .

I feel big because
I can fly.

I dream big because
I am an artist.

I play big because
I am fierce.

I sing big because I am happy.

I swing big because I am brave.

I love big because
I am loved.

I am me...

...and I am...

BIG!